Presented To:

_____

From:

_____

Date:

_____

Baby's First
Book of Prayers

BY MELODY CARLSON
ILLUSTRATED BY JUDITH PFEIFFER

ZONDERkidz™
.com

Zonderkidz

Baby's First Book of Prayers
Copyright © 2002 by Melody Carlson
Illustrations copyright © 2002 by Judith Pfeiffer

Requests for information should be addressed to:
Zonderkidz, 3900 Sparks Drive SE
Grand Rapids, Michigan 49546

ISBN: 978-0-310-70287-0

Zonderkidz is a trademark of Zondervan.

Editor: Gwen Ellis
Art Direction: Michelle Lenger

Printed in China
24 DSC 46

To the newborn babies who lost loved
ones in the September 11th crisis.

May your Heavenly Father keep you safe in
his loving hands, and watch over you always.

-M.C.

Contents

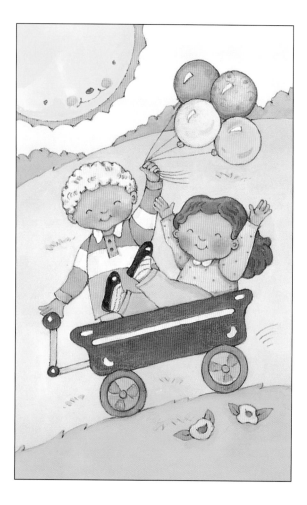

This New Day

Thank you, God, for this great day!

The sun is up, and I must say,

I'm as happy as can be

For each new day you give to me.

Amen

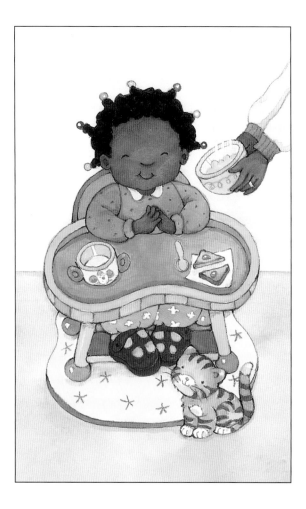

Thank You for My Breakfast

There's a rumble in my tummy,

I smell something that smells yummy!

I see breakfast. It looks good.

Thank you, God! Please, bless my food.

Amen

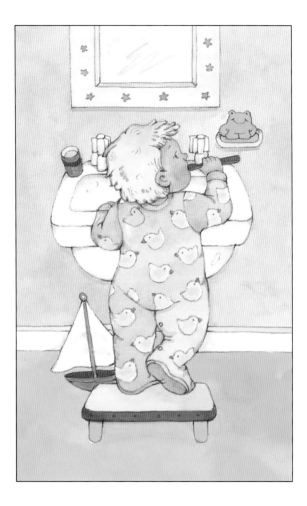

Step by Step

I learn something new each day,

Step by step along my way.

Thank you, God, for how I grow,

And thank you for the things I know.

Amen

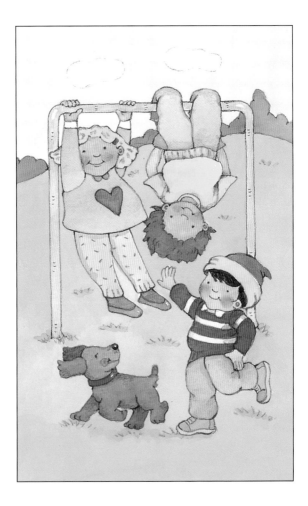

Bless Me as I Play

I love to laugh! And I love fun!

I can romp and I can run,

I can jump and skip all day.

Bless me, God, while I'm at play.

Amen

The Green, Green Grass

Good for rolling and bare toes,

The green, green grass grows and grows!

Thank you, God, for this fine treat,

Soft and cushy 'neath my feet!

Amen

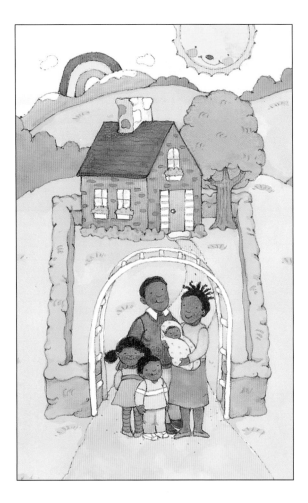

Bless My Home

Bless my home, dear God, I pray,

Keep it safe by night and day.

Bless each room and bless each wall.

Bless my family. Bless us all!

Amen

I Am Getting Bigger

When I stretch my hands up high,

I can almost reach the sky.

I am growing tall and straight.

Thank you, God! You're really great!

Amen

Bless Mommy

She shows me how to tie my shoe,

And gives good hugs and kisses too.

She cares for me, and all the rest.

God bless Mommy, she's the best!

Amen

Thank You for the Sun

The sunlight shines across my bed.

It wakes me up. It warms my head.

It makes my world a lot more fun.

Thank you, God, for your bright sun!

Amen

Thank You for My Nose

Thank you, God, for eyes that see

And ears that listen carefully.

Thank you, God, for my smart nose,

It knows a pickle from a rose.

Amen

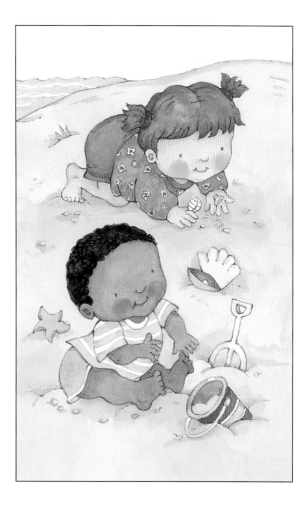

Fingers and Toes

Fingers do so many things–

Pick up pennies and wear rings.

God made toes to help us stand,

And to wiggle in the sand.

Amen

Thank You for Laughter

Giggles gurgle in my tummy

Each time I see something funny.

Laughing is more fun than toys.

Thank you, God, for happy joys!

Amen

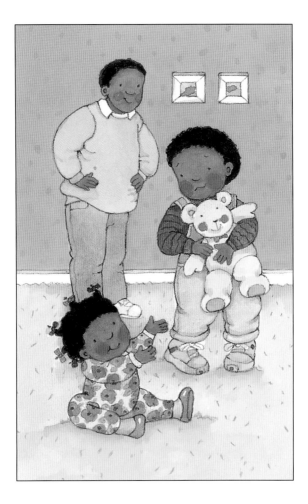

Help Me to Share

Even though I try to mind,

I'm not always very kind.

I know it's right to give and care.

Help me, God. Teach me to share.

Amen

Thank You for Flowers

Thank you, God, for birds and bees.

Thank you, God, for cherry trees.

Thank you, God, for springtime showers.

Thank you, God, for pretty flowers.

Amen

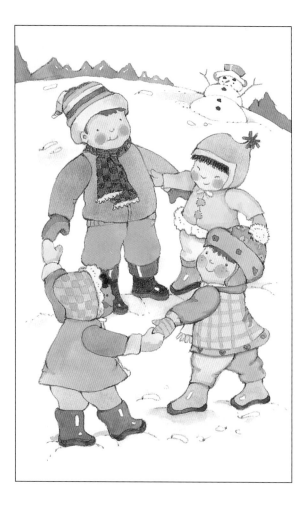

Bless My Friends

I visit friends so we can play.

I wish that I could stay all day.

I like my friends, both short and tall.

God, bless my friends.

Please bless them all!

Amen

I'm Sorry, God

Sometimes I do something bad,

And it makes you very sad.

I'm as sorry as can be.

Thank you for forgiving me.

Amen

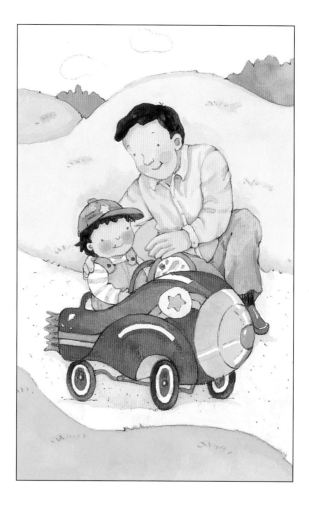

On the Go

I like wheels and things that go-

Zipping fast or cruising slow.

In a rocket, or a sleigh,

God, bless us as we go our way!

Amen

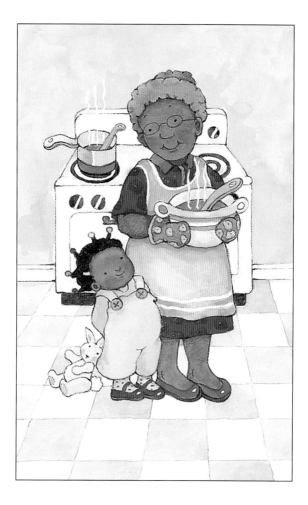

Thank You for My Lunch

It always happens, every day,

I eat something, then I play.

Today it's soup, I have a hunch.

Thank you, God, I like my lunch!

Amen

Thank You for the Rain

Huge clouds, like pillows, fill the sky,

Full of tears, they weep and cry.

And even though it seems a pain,

I thank you, God, for sending rain.

Amen

Help Me to Be Kind

Please, help me to do what I should,

To love and share and to be good,

To care for others and be kinder,

I may need a good reminder.

Amen

Wiggles and Giggles

Thank you, God, for toes that wiggle

And ticklish tummies that can giggle.

Thank you, God, for silly things

Like clowns and jokes and slinky springs!

Amen

When I Am Sad

Sometimes when my heart feels bad,

And I'm feeling very sad,

Even if I shed a tear,

I still know that God is here.

Amen

Thank You for My Toys

Thank you, God, for stuff that's fun,

Balls and blocks and things that run.

When I'm done each day with play,

I'll thank you for this happy day.

Amen

Thank You for Rest Time

I love to hop and jump and go,

I never want the fun to slow.

But I guess you know what's best,

Thank you, God, for giving rest.

Amen

Bless Daddy

I love when Daddy carries me,

Like I'm flying fast and free,

Or when we dance a funny jig.

Bless my Daddy. Bless him big!

Amen

Thanks for Hugs

Some hugs are squishy, stiff, or strong.

Some are short and some are long.

Some are cozy, warm, and snug.

Thank you, God, for making hugs!

Amen

My Happy Heart

Sometimes I want to sing and shout.

I want to let my feelings out.

Thank you, God, for loving me—

And now I'll sing so happily!

Amen

Funny Faces

I can wink or grin or frown,

Or act goofy, like a clown.

Thank you, God, for this great face.

'Cause I can take it everyplace!

Amen

Creepy Critters

Thank you, God, for bugs that crawl.

Some are long and some are small.

Some have wings and some are hairy.

Some are big and sort of scary.

Amen

Thank You for Smiles

Thank you, God, for happy smiles.

Some can last for miles and miles.

It's good to take a smile with you

To share with someone who feels blue.

Amen

In Your Big Hands

The world is big. I know it's true.

But, God, it's not too big for you.

In your big hands, we all can rest

You keep us safe. You do what's best.

Amen

The Birds That Sing

I love to hear the robins sing,

Or chickadees a' chickering.

They sail around the sky of blue

And chirp to God, "How we love you!"

Amen

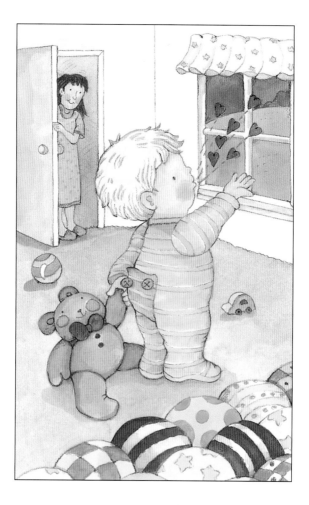

Blowing a Kiss

Sometimes it looks like I'm alone,

But, God, you're right here too.

I tell you just how great you are,

And blow a kiss to you!

Amen

Thank You for My Dinner

Thank you, God, for food to eat.

It tastes so good. Oh, what a treat!

Bless our meal, dear God, I pray,

And thank you for this special day.

Amen

Handy Hands

Hands sure come in handy

For finger paint and candy,

And for counting-fingers go to ten.

Thank you, God, for all of them!

Amen

Watch Over Me

God, I know that you can see

Everything–and you see me!

And even if I have a scare

I know I'm safe within your care.

Amen

Furry Things

Thank you, God, for things with fur,

Things with tails and things that purr.

I love puppies, cats, and mice,

And guinea pigs are really nice!

Amen

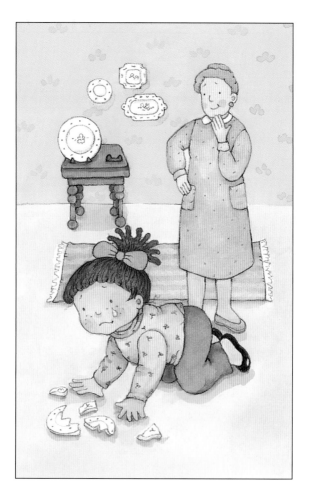

When Tears Fall

Things don't always go just right,

Sometimes there's trouble or a fight.

I trust you, God, when teardrops fall,

I know that you can dry them all.

Amen

The Moon and Stars

I thank you, God, for quiet night,

For the silver moon so big and bright.

For the starry sky and each bright spark.

For keeping our world from being dark.

Amen

Thank You for My Bed

At night I am a sleepyhead,

And I am thankful for my bed.

I pray, dear God, you'll send moonbeams,

And give me good and pleasant dreams!

Amen

Good Night, God

Good night, dear God, now I must sleep,

I'll close my eyes and slumber deep.

I know you watch me from above,

And cover me with your sweet love.

Amen